THE BOXCAR CHILDREN MYSTERIES

THE BOXCAR CHILDREN
SURPRISE ISLAND
THE YELLOW HOUSE MYSTERY
MYSTERY RANCH
MIKE'S MYSTERY
BLUE BAY MYSTERY
THE WOODSHED MYSTERY
THE LIGHTHOUSE MYSTERY
MOUNTAIN TOP MYSTERY
SCHOOLHOUSE MYSTERY
CABOOSE MYSTERY
HOUSEBOAT MYSTERY
SNOWBOUND MYSTERY
TREE HOUSE MYSTERY
BICYCLE MYSTERY
MYSTERY IN THE SAND
MYSTERY BEHIND THE WALL
BUS STATION MYSTERY
BENNY UNCOVERS A MYSTERY
THE HAUNTED CABIN MYSTERY
THE DESERTED LIBRARY MYSTERY
THE ANIMAL SHELTER MYSTERY
THE OLD MOTEL MYSTERY
THE MYSTERY OF THE HIDDEN PAINTING
THE AMUSEMENT PARK MYSTERY
THE MYSTERY OF THE MIXED-UP ZOO
THE CAMP-OUT MYSTERY
THE MYSTERY GIRL
THE MYSTERY CRUISE
THE DISAPPEARING FRIEND MYSTERY
THE MYSTERY OF THE SINGING GHOST
THE MYSTERY IN THE SNOW
THE PIZZA MYSTERY
THE MYSTERY HORSE
THE MYSTERY AT THE DOG SHOW
THE CASTLE MYSTERY
THE MYSTERY OF THE LOST VILLAGE
THE MYSTERY ON THE ICE
THE MYSTERY OF THE PURPLE POOL
THE GHOST SHIP MYSTERY
THE MYSTERY IN WASHINGTON, DC
THE CANOE TRIP MYSTERY
THE MYSTERY OF THE HIDDEN BEACH
THE MYSTERY OF THE MISSING CAT
THE MYSTERY AT SNOWFLAKE INN

THE MYSTERY ON STAGE
THE DINOSAUR MYSTERY
THE MYSTERY OF THE STOLEN MUSIC
THE MYSTERY AT THE BALL PARK
THE CHOCOLATE SUNDAE MYSTERY
THE MYSTERY OF THE HOT AIR BALLOON
THE MYSTERY BOOKSTORE
THE PILGRIM VILLAGE MYSTERY
THE MYSTERY OF THE STOLEN BOXCAR
THE MYSTERY IN THE CAVE
THE MYSTERY ON THE TRAIN
THE MYSTERY AT THE FAIR
THE MYSTERY OF THE LOST MINE
THE GUIDE DOG MYSTERY
THE HURRICANE MYSTERY
THE PET SHOP MYSTERY
THE MYSTERY OF THE SECRET MESSAGE
THE FIREHOUSE MYSTERY
THE MYSTERY IN SAN FRANCISCO
THE NIAGARA FALLS MYSTERY
THE MYSTERY AT THE ALAMO
THE OUTER SPACE MYSTERY
THE SOCCER MYSTERY
THE MYSTERY IN THE OLD ATTIC
THE GROWLING BEAR MYSTERY
THE MYSTERY OF THE LAKE MONSTER
THE MYSTERY AT PEACOCK HALL
THE WINDY CITY MYSTERY
THE BLACK PEARL MYSTERY
THE CEREAL BOX MYSTERY
THE PANTHER MYSTERY
THE MYSTERY OF THE QUEEN'S JEWELS
THE STOLEN SWORD MYSTERY
THE BASKETBALL MYSTERY
THE MOVIE STAR MYSTERY
THE MYSTERY OF THE PIRATE'S MAP
THE GHOST TOWN MYSTERY
THE MYSTERY OF THE BLACK RAVEN
THE MYSTERY IN THE MALL
THE MYSTERY IN NEW YORK
THE GYMNASTICS MYSTERY
THE POISON FROG MYSTERY
THE MYSTERY OF THE EMPTY SAFE
THE HOME RUN MYSTERY
THE GREAT BICYCLE RACE MYSTERY

THE BOXCAR CHILDREN®

CREATED BY
GERTRUDE CHANDLER WARNER

BOOK

157

SCIENCE FAIR SABOTAGE

ILLUSTRATED BY
ANTHONY VanARSDALE

ALBERT WHITMAN & COMPANY
CHICAGO, ILLINOIS

Printed in the United States of America
10 9 8 7 6 5 4 3 2 1 LB 24 23 22 21 20

Illustrations by Anthony VanArsdale

Visit The Boxcar Children® online at www.boxcarchildren.com.
For more information about Albert Whitman & Company,
visit our website at www.albertwhitman.com.

Contents

River Ride

"My arms are tired." Six-year-old Benny Alden set his paddle across his legs. "I don't want to row anymore."

"Benny, we need your paddle in the water to keep the canoe straight," said Henry from the back of the boat. At fourteen, he was the oldest of the four children. "You're an important part of Team Alden."

Still, Benny didn't put his paddle in the water.

Jessie spoke up from her seat in the front of the canoe. She was twelve and always seemed to know just what to tell her little brother. "This is the roughest patch of the river, Benny. Remember, there's a big meal waiting at the end."

At the mention of food, Benny pushed his sweat-soaked hair from his forehead. He flexed his muscles and said, "I'll do it for Team Alden!"

But before Benny could do a thing, the river's current pulled the canoe sideways.

"Watch out!" Ten-year-old Violet called. She had been taking pictures of the scenery with her new digital camera. Now, she picked up her paddle.

Ahead, a glistening boulder stuck high out of the water. If the children didn't steer around it, the canoe would flip and dump them all into the river.

"Smash alert!" Benny shrieked. "Crash position!" He ducked down and put his head between his legs.

"No need to panic. We just need to paddle together," Henry said. He called, "Stroke! Stroke! Stroke!" The three oldest Aldens worked double time to turn the boat back on course. Before long, the rock was behind them.

"Whew," said Violet, smoothing out her ponytail. "That was close."

"I was so scared!" said Benny. Then he added, "I think we all deserve a snack. Is there a cooler hiding somewhere?"

"Sorry," Henry said. "This is a short trip, remember? Grandfather is waiting for us."

It was a late summer day, and the children were enjoying the last of the warm weather by canoeing down the Greenfield River. At the end of their route, they planned to meet Grandfather for lunch at Greenfield's Lookout Café.

Jessie, Violet, Henry, and Benny had not always lived with their grandfather. After their parents died, the children had run away. They'd heard that Grandfather Alden was mean and were afraid to live with him. They had found shelter in an old boxcar in the woods, and, for a short time, made it their home. The children had all kinds of adventures in the boxcar. When Grandfather had found them, they discovered he wasn't mean at all and came to live with him. The children still had all kinds of adventures.

"How much longer, Henry?" Benny asked. He added, "Do you have a sandwich in your life jacket pocket?"

"Life jackets don't have pockets, silly," Henry chuckled.

Violet pulled the straps to tighten the orange vest around her middle. "It's good we were wearing life jackets," she said. "We almost tipped over."

"It's important to be prepared," said Henry. "Sometimes things happen that no one can control."

"It's important to be prepared," Benny repeated. He thought for a long moment then said, "I think I'll make a life jacket with a special pocket for a sandwich." He added, "I'm going to invent a machine that rows the boat for me too." He went on, "Then, we need an air conditioning umbrella to cool us down. A waterproof boat pillow to rest my sleepy head." Benny's eyes got big as he added another idea to the list. "And a special doggy seat for Watch!"

Watch was the name of the Aldens' wirehaired terrier. The man who rented the canoe to them had said no dogs were allowed. So Watch was waiting with Grandfather at the end of the route.

Benny had been upset not to bring Watch along. Now, he was excited about his idea. "I could make a doggy life vest too!" He clapped his hands. "With a pocket for dog treats!"

"You are full of good ideas," said Jessie. "Maybe I should use one for my science fair project."

All summer, Jessie had been looking forward to joining her school's Science Fair Club. In the club's first meeting, she had partnered with Claudia Tobin, who had won the competition the year before. Jessie was excited to have such a smart partner. Now, they just needed to find the perfect project.

"You're going to invent a dog life vest, Jessie?" Violet asked, brown eyes wide with surprise.

"With a treat pocket," Benny added. "That's the most important part."

Jessie giggled. "I don't think Claudia would want to make a dog vest."

"You've only had one meeting," Henry said. "The perfect idea will come to you."

For a few minutes, the children were quiet as they paddled around a bend. Henry convinced Benny to help by promising him *two* sandwiches at the end of the trip.

"And ice cream?" Benny asked before putting his oar into the water.

"I'd never forget dessert," said Henry.

Before long, the children came to a calm area where they could float along. Violet took a picture of a mallard duck that Benny spotted. And two turtles Henry pointed out.

But Jessie was still thinking about her science fair project. "Claudia and I want to do something that will make a difference," she said. "We have to decide soon so we can get busy doing the research."

"You'll find your project," said Benny. "I'm a hundred and two percent positive."

"I've got my fingers crossed one hundred and two times," Jessie joked.

"It's nice we have this river and so much nature this close to Greenfield," said Violet, peering through her camera lens. "Maybe there's a river project you could do, Jessie?"

"I wonder..." Jessie began to think about it.

Violet aimed her camera toward the shore and squinted through the lens. "Hey, what's going on over there?"

"What do you see?" asked Henry.

"It looks like construction," Violet said.

As the boat got closer, the children saw a tall metal fence blocking off the work site from the river. Loud clanging noises came from the other side.

"That's strange," said Jessie. "I didn't think anyone could build by the river—not after the Big Cleanup."

"Big Cleanup?" Benny asked.

"That's right," said Henry. "A while back, there was a big effort to clean up the Greenfield River. At the time, there were no birds. The water smelled weird. Everyone used to joke there was so much pollution in the river that the fish had three eyes."

"Mutant fish!" said Benny. He peeked over the side of the canoe to see if he could find any strange creatures. "I thought falling in the water would be bad. Swimming with mutant fishes would be..." He thought about the right word, then said, "Really bad!"

"Those are just rumors, Benny." Jessie pointed to a fishing dock on the side of the river, where a man and his daughter were holding fishing rods. The girl had a fish hanging from a hook. "See? Nothing to worry about."

"Don't eat that!" Benny shouted. "It might have extra eyeballs!"

"We need to paddle," said Henry, changing the subject. The end of the river ride was coming up, and the children needed to get to the right side of the riverbank. "All together, Team Alden! Stroke. Stroke. Stroke."

Still, as Jessie paddled along, she couldn't help but look at the water and wonder: Had things really changed for the Greenfield River?

CHAPTER 2

Change of Plans

"Sandwich time!" Benny said as the canoe pulled onto the sandy shore.

"We need to return the boat first," said Henry.

"Oh bother," Benny groaned. He looked down the path leading to the Lookout Café. "They're so close I can smell them."

"We'll be there soon," said Jessie, hopping out and pulling the canoe onto the sandy shore.

Once all the children were out, Benny sniffed the air. "The whole menu is attacking my nose. There are sandwiches and cookies and apples." Benny sneezed. "And chocolate ice cream for dessert!"

"You have a super-sniffer," Violet said with a laugh. She snapped a photo of Benny licking his lips.

Change of Plans

The children pulled the canoe all the way onto the shore. At the landing, a red pickup truck with a trailer full of kayaks and canoes was parked.

Benny sounded out the words on the side of the truck. "'Cho's the Best Choice.'" Benny tilted his head. "We got our canoe from Mr. Cho, but the sign at his shack had another name."

Jessie nodded. "You're right, Benny. Mr. Cho's business is called Lazy River Rentals. 'Cho's the Best Choice' is his motto."

"What does that mean?" Benny asked.

"A motto is a phrase that helps people remember your business," said Henry. "Mr. Cho wants people to know his shop is the best choice."

"But it's the *only* choice," said Violet.

Henry shrugged. "I guess that makes it the best."

"Well," said Benny, "if I were him, my motto would be Lazy River Rentals: There's Food at the End."

With that, Mr. Cho stepped out of his vehicle. The man wore sandals, cargo shorts, and a Lazy River Rentals polo shirt. He had long, dark hair under a blue baseball cap, and was stretching like he had just woken up from a nap. "Right on time," he said. "You can set it next to the others, please."

Henry shared a confused look with Jessie. "Huh?" he asked.

"On the rack," said Mr. Cho, pointing to the trailer loaded high with kayaks and canoes.

"Oh. Sure thing," said Henry. He was surprised that Mr. Cho expected them to move the canoe all by themselves. But he didn't want to be rude. "Everyone grab an edge. Jessie and Violet on one side. I'll take the other side with Benny."

"Righto!" said Benny. "The faster we return the boat, the faster we..." He sniffed the air. "You know..." Benny's belly rumbled.

Henry rubbed Benny's head. "You can call the march," he said. "Like I did with the paddle strokes."

"I'm the boat-walking boss!" Benny cheered. He told his siblings, "Team Alden. Heave-ho." He explained, "That means lift the boat."

Once the boat was off the ground, Benny said, "Team Alden. Left foot forward." Then, "Right foot." Then, "Left foot."

As Benny called out the march, Henry wondered if they should put the canoe anyplace in particular. But Mr. Cho did not seem to care. He was still yawning and stretching next to his pickup.

"Team Alden. Stop-ho. Team Alden. Lower-ho!" Benny called. Then explained, "That means put down the boat."

The children placed the canoe onto the open space on the rack, then turned to Mr. Cho. "Thanks for the canoe," said Henry. "We had a great time."

"Want to go back and start again?" Mr. Cho asked. "I could give you a little discount for a second trip."

"No, thank you," Benny said. He'd already started up the path to the café. "My tummy's leading us on a new adventure."

Mr. Cho shrugged. "Well, I had to ask. Business has been slow these days." He pulled out a strap to secure the canoe. But instead of hooking it up himself, he handed it to Henry. Henry knew how to tie knots. Still, he was surprised Mr. Cho would trust him to secure the canoe to the trailer.

"Why do you think business hasn't been good

lately?" Violet asked.

"Is it because of the mutant fishes?" asked Benny.

"I think what he means is, do you think the water has anything to do with it?" Jessie explained.

"The water? Oh no. This river is perfectly clean!" said Mr. Cho. "After the Big Cleanup, I thought all kinds of people would want rides down the river. So I bought the old rental shack. But business has been awfully slow."

Henry finished putting the strap on the trailer. Mr. Cho gave it a pull to test its tightness and nodded. On his way back to his truck, he added, "Sometimes I wonder if I'm on the right river at all. But what can you do?" With that, he got in his truck and drove away.

After Mr. Cho had gone, the Aldens headed down the path to the Lookout Café. The restaurant was the last stop for kayakers, fishers, and bird watchers visiting the river. Just beyond the old-fashioned wood and stone building, the river dropped into a small but fast-moving waterfall. The falls were very pretty, but impossible to float through.

The children seated themselves on the crowded

outdoor patio. "This is the perfect place to look out over the river," said Jessie.

"Just like the name says," said Violet. From the railing, she took a photo of the rainbow from the mist of the falls.

The restaurant owner, Mrs. Fernando, came by to tell them Grandfather had just stepped away. He needed to take Watch for a quick walk.

Benny groaned.

"The good news," Mrs. Fernando added, "is he left you some money. And a little extra in case any of you are extra hungry." Mrs. Fernando winked at Benny.

Without looking at the menu, Benny blurted out his order, which included two sandwiches and a dessert. After everyone had placed their orders, the children relaxed from their paddle in the cool, refreshing breeze coming over the waterfall.

Before long, Mrs. Fernando arrived with their food. Jessie thanked her and said, "Your business seems to be doing really well since the Big Cleanup."

Mrs. Fernando sighed. "Yes, it has come a long way from those days. We have done a lot of advertising to help get people back here. We get our water from the city, just like everyone else. But people don't like to look out over a river they think is dirty, especially when they're eating."

"Well, it's a good thing you have nothing to worry about," said Violet. "Now that river is all cleaned up."

Mrs. Fernando nodded. "The rules the city put in place because of the Big Cleanup helped a lot," she said. "They pushed farmers' fields farther away from the river, so they didn't pollute the water. And they made it so no new buildings could be built close to the riverbank."

Benny swallowed a big bite of sandwich and said, "I have a question! If there are no new buildings allowed, what about the construction fence we saw and the sounds we heard?" He imitated the sound of an engine. "It sounded like big trucks and metal."

"You know, I have wondered about that too. I was told that there's going to be a nice pathway leading from downtown to the river." She sighed. "A new path would be good for business."

"But?" Jessie asked. "You don't seem happy about that."

"I'm worried about people trying to get around the rules." Mrs. Fernando glanced toward the waterfall. "The last thing we need around here is another Big Cleanup."

Just then, someone called from the kitchen with another order.

"I need to run," she said. But before she did, she leaned over and said softly, so no one else could hear, "I know you Aldens like a mystery. I've noticed the water near here has been a little...stinky lately. The color seems murkier than normal too. Maybe you can figure out what's going on." With that, she dashed off to the kitchen.

"Stinky, murky water?!" Benny exclaimed. He turned to Violet. "Check my toes. Do I have webbing like a frog?" He began to pull off his shoes.

"Keep your sneakers on," Violet told him. "There's no reason to worry." She looked to Henry. "Right? We're not worried?"

"My toes do feel a little funny," Henry teased his little brother. "They tingle!"

"Don't joke." Benny gave his brother a look. "Mutating is very serious."

"So is bad water," Violet said. "Very, very serious. Right, Jessie?"

Jessie nodded at her sister. "It is. And finding the solution could make a big difference."

***

At the next after-school Science Fair Club meeting, Jessie couldn't wait to tell Claudia about her idea for their project. But when she walked into the classroom, Claudia wasn't there.

"Do you know where Claudia is?" Jessie asked Ms. Kennedy, the science teacher in charge of the club.

"I haven't seen her today," Ms. Kennedy said, pushing up her glasses and looking at the sign-in sheet. "Have you two decided on a project yet?"

"I have an idea," Jessie told the teacher. "I was hoping to tell Claudia—"

"I'm so sorry I'm late," Claudia said, rushing into the room and over to Jessie's lab table. She had on overalls and muddy work boots. "What were you hoping to tell me?"

Jessie knew Claudia loved being outdoors and wondered where she'd been, but she was too excited to ask. "I think I have the perfect project for us," she said.

A big smile appeared on Claudia's face. "Really? I want to hear all about it!"

Jessie knew Claudia would be excited, so she jumped right in. "Well, like Ms. Kennedy always says, all good science projects start with a question. Last weekend I was canoeing with my brothers and sister, and we found the perfect question! Mrs. Fernando at the Lookout Café thinks the water smells funny. And Mr. Cho says people aren't coming to do his river rides. So we want to figure out if the Greenfield River really is clean."

"That sounds like a wonderful project!" Ms. Kennedy said. "You know, before I was a science teacher, I studied the environment. Clean water is one of the most important things in the world. I would be happy to help advise you." She added, "But this is a big project. Are you sure you two can handle it?"

"Yes!" Jessie cheered.

At the same time, Claudia shouted, "No!"

"What?" Jessie turned to Claudia. "I thought you would like this project. It's outdoors, and I think we have a chance to really make a difference."

"I did," Claudia said. "I mean, I do..." She dug the toe of her boot against the tile floor. "I just—I don't want to study the river." Claudia had dark, curly hair. She looped a curl around a finger. "If the city said the water was clean after the Big Cleanup, I don't think we need to test it."

"But—" Jessie began. "What if something is changing?"

"I'm sorry," said Claudia. "I just don't want to study the river."

"Well," Ms. Kennedy stepped back from the girls. "Looks like you two have a lot to talk about. Teachers are not allowed to get very involved in the science fair. I can advise you, but only after you pick a project. Even then, I can't help much." She put a hand on Jessie's arm. "When you figure out a plan, let me know."

Ms. Kennedy walked away.

Jessie was confused. She thought for sure

Claudia would be excited about their experiment. Still, it was important that she and Claudia were both happy. "Okay, we'll think of something else then," Jessie said. "Have you had a chance to come up with any ideas? I can keep thinking. My brothers and sister and I are great at finding questions that need to be answered."

At this, Claudia only seemed to get more upset. "I don't think we should work together," she said.

Jessie's heart sank. "I don't understand," she said. "I thought we were a team."

"Sorry. I think it's better if I work on my own," Claudia said. With that, she went to tell Ms. Kennedy her decision.

Jessie stood at the back of the room, watching other students talk about their science fair projects. There was no way she could do the project all by herself.

What was she going to do?

CHAPTER 3

Stink and Murk

Jessie sat at her desk in the boxcar. It was the place where she did her best thinking. And she had a lot to think about.

Benny was resting in the beanbag chair, waiting for Henry and Violet to come back from the kitchen. Mrs. McGregor, the family's housekeeper, was on vacation, so the children had helped Grandfather cook supper and clean up. Now it was time for studying and snacks.

"What are you reading, Jessie?" Benny asked, moving over to let Watch join him in his beanbag. "Are you and Claudia going to study mutant fish?" He squeezed his lips together and blew her a fishy kiss.

Jessie sighed. "No. I'm looking for a different project." Jessie hadn't wanted to ruin supper with her bad news. Now, she told Benny, "Claudia wants to do a different project. I have to find one I can do on my own."

"Claudia didn't want to study the river?" Violet asked. She carried a bag of sliced apples and some boxes of raisins into the clubhouse.

Henry had a pitcher of juice and glasses. He set them down on an upside-down crate. "Why can't you study the river on your own?"

"Ms. Kennedy says it's too big a project for one person." Jessie gave another big, rumbling sigh. She was full of sighs.

Benny took a handful of raisins and stuffed them into his mouth. Then he jumped up from the beanbag, causing Watch to jump to the floor. "Weeecanelp."

"Benny!" Violet pointed a finger at him. "Swallow first!"

Benny made a big show of swallowing his snack. Then he said, "We can help!"

"I wish." Jessie turned her chair to look at her

brother. "We don't go to the same school, Benny."

"But we're Team Alden. Remember?" Benny said, stepping between Henry and Violet. "We survived giant rocks and mutant fishes, so we can do anything!"

"He's right," Henry said. "Well...mostly right. There's got to be a way."

Jessie thought for a moment. "Maybe..." she began. "If I do the science fair part, like analyzing the data, we should be okay."

"I will take photos for your poster board!" said Violet.

"I can help collect samples," Henry said.

"And I'll bring sandwiches," Benny added. "Can Watch help too?"

"Of course," said Jessie, feeling her mood lift. Watch came by her chair, and she scratched his neck. "We can use all the help we can get."

***

On Saturday, Team Alden gathered the supplies for their science fair experiment. Jessie had spoken with Ms. Kennedy about her family helping her, and Ms. Kennedy had said that as long as Jessie did all of the testing, analyzing, and presenting, her family was more than welcome to be involved. Ms. Kennedy had also given Jessie papers to read about planning the experiment.

While Grandfather drove the children to the first testing spot, Violet looked at the supplies in the back seat. There were washbasins and chest waders and glass jars and what looked like a big butterfly net. "Why do we need a net?" Violet asked.

"Are we going to go fishing for mutant fishes?" Benny asked.

"That would be a big problem," Henry said. "I think we're looking for smaller changes. Right, Jessie?"

"Right," said Jessie. She told the others what Ms. Kennedy had told her. "The tricky thing about testing water is that the river is always flowing. That means the water is always changing."

Violet scrunched up her eyebrows. "If the water keeps moving, there might be bad stuff in the river we miss," she said. "So how will we know if the water is good?"

"Do we have to stay all day long?" asked Benny.

He looked at his tote bag full of snacks. "I don't think we packed enough for that."

Jessie smiled. "No, Benny. *We* don't need to stay all day. But the way to find out if the water is good is to test the things that *do* stay in the river all day."

Grandfather turned onto the road that led to the Lookout Café. Jessie had decided to take the first samples at the café because it was where Mrs. Fernando had noticed the changes. She planned to take samples from three spots, then check the same locations later to see if things had changed.

"The project is not just about fish," Jessie continued. "There are all kinds of critters that live in the river."

"Critters?" Violet asked. "Are they dangerous?" She didn't like the idea of creatures she didn't know about in the water.

"They're harmless," said Jessie. "They are things like snails and worms and crabs. The more there are, the cleaner the water is. If there are no critters, or just a few, it's a sign that something bad is happening. Nothing wants to live in bad water."

Benny shoved his tote bag toward Violet. "All

this talk about critters is making my stomach feel yucky." He sat for a long minute then took his lunch back and peeked in at his snacks. "Okay, I feel better now."

Grandfather pulled into the parking lot of the Lookout Café. The children collected their supplies and walked toward the patio, where stairs led down to the river.

Mrs. Fernando waved and smiled from the patio. But when the children turned to go down the steps to the river instead of to the restaurant, she looked confused. Others on the patio looked curiously at the Aldens' supplies.

"We must look strange with all this stuff," said Henry.

"It's okay," said Jessie. "We look weird for science!"

On the bank of the river, Jessie and Henry each put on a pair of Grandfather's chest waders. They were much too big. But both Henry and Jessie were able to pull the straps so they could walk without tripping.

"Move slowly," Jessie told her brother. "It's

slippery in the river."

The two entered the water in a calm area just past the patio deck. The falls were to their left, but they kept far enough away to stay out of the spray.

Violet and Benny stood on the shore. "It does smell a little strange," she said, taking a big sniff. "Not too bad. Just kind of funny."

From the riverbank, Watch gave a snort.

"Watch agrees," said Benny. "I'm a good sniffer, but dogs are experts."

"Does it look like the color is different?" Violet asked.

"I can't tell," Jessie said. "It's not crystal clear blue, but it's not muddy brown either."

Jessie took a glass jar and filled it with water. "We need to take a closer look. We'll take a sample of the water each time so we can know if the water is changing."

Jessie handed the jar to Benny, who took out a piece of masking tape and a marker. He paused.

"How do you spell 'Lookout'?" he asked Violet. But by the time Violet was done spelling, Benny had just gotten the cap off of the marker. "I'll just put a letter *L* for *Lookout* and 1 for number one." He wrote the label on the tape and stuck it to the jar.

"Now we need to take our other sample. Right, Jessie?" Henry said, holding the big net.

Jessie nodded and picked up a washbasin. Together they waded into the stream. When they were far enough in, Jessie made a note of the location in her notebook. Then they both started shaking their hips and marching in place.

"Are you doing a fish dance?" said Benny. "Is that part of the test?" Benny shook his hips and wiggled his head like a fish would.

Jessie laughed. "No, Benny. For the experiment to work, we need to loosen up the soil with our feet. That way we can scoop out a good sample."

Benny shrugged. He kept doing his own dance.

Henry dumped a net full of muck into the washbasin Jessie was carrying. Then they came ashore. Jessie handed her notebook to Violet and looked down into the washbasin.

"Now comes the fun part," said Jessie. Slowly, she poured more water into the washbasin. As she did, little critters appeared out of the muck. One by

one, she scooped them out and into another clean washbasin. It was slow, messy work.

"Here's what I see," Jessie told her sister when she was done sorting through the muck. "Three worms. Four crawdads. Eight water bugs, and one snail."

Violet wrote down the count of each type of critter. When they were done, Jessie dumped the basin back into the water so the creatures could go back to their homes.

As the children walked up the steps back to the patio, a man shouted, "Hey, is the water okay?" He held up a drinking glass. "Should I be worried?"

Before Jessie could answer, Mrs. Fernando hurried over. "What do you think you are doing here?" she asked.

"We're testing the water for my science fair experiment," said Jessie. "I thought you wanted us to figure out what was going on."

Mrs. Fernando shook her head. "The problem isn't here," she said. "It's up the river!"

"We don't know that yet," said Jessie. "That is why we are testing."

Mrs. Fernando looked back at the curious

customers on her patio. "Well, I don't want you doing any more of this 'experiment' on my property." With that, she stormed away.

Jessie looked at her brothers and sister. Mrs. Fernando was the one who had given Jessie the idea for her project. Didn't she want her to find out what was going on?

***

The Aldens' second stop was at the fishing dock, which was right across the river from a large farm field. Part of Jessie's project was to figure out, if there was pollution, where it was coming from. Ms. Kennedy had told her that farm fields had caused a lot of pollution in the past from fertilizer and other chemicals. Jessie wanted to see if there might still be a problem.

Next to the dock, Jessie found five worms, six crawdads, ten water bugs, four snails, and a beetle.

Then she scooped a jar full of water and passed it to Benny.

Benny wrote an *F* for *fishing dock* and a *1* for the first sample. Just as Jessie and Henry were about to get out of their waders, a man on the dock stopped them. "Say," the man said. "Do you think you could do me a favor? My line is stuck." He held up his fishing pole to show he could not pull his line back in.

"Sure," said Henry. "I can help you get your line unstuck."

Henry stepped into the water and followed the line into the river. He moved slowly because the river bottom was slippery. Toward the middle, the water came up almost to the top of his waders. But as he crossed toward the other bank, the water became shallower.

Violet took photos as Henry reached the end of the fishing line.

"It's tangled on a pipe," Henry said, leaning over to get a better grip. He waded a little further into the river. He was curious. Over the ripple of the river current, there was another noise he hadn't noticed before.

A pumping sound.

If he wasn't listening hard, he might never have heard it. Henry freed the fisherman's line and started back to where the others were waiting. He reported to Jessie, Violet, and Benny what he'd seen and heard.

"Why is there a pump in the river?" Jessie asked. She wrote a note down in her notebook. "One end is in the water. Where is the other?"

"Do you think the pump could be the thing making the water smelly?" asked Violet.

"And murky," Benny added. "Don't forget murky. Mrs. Fernando said there was both stink and murk."

"We won't forget, Benny," Jessie said. "I have a feeling if we find the answer to one, we will find the answer to the other."

Weirder and Weirder

Jessie's third and final testing site was near Lazy River Rentals. To get to the rental shop from the fishing dock, Grandfather had to drive all the way around the construction site.

"It keeps going and going," said Benny, looking at the tall, chain-link fence that surrounded the property. The fence was covered by a dark fabric so no one could see what was happening behind it. "I wonder what's going on back there."

"Whatever it is, it's awfully loud," said Violet, closing the car window to block out the sound of clanging metal and the buzz of heavy equipment.

Over the top of the fence, Henry saw a machine with a huge shovel for digging. "Didn't Mrs.

Fernando say they were building a pathway from Greenfield to the river?" he asked.

"She did," said Jessie. "I wonder why they are digging so much for a path. Can't they just smooth the land and put down cement or gravel?" She admitted she didn't know much about making paths.

Grandfather slowed the car. They were reaching the end of the construction zone. The route had taken them all the way to the edge of downtown Greenfield. Henry looked at one of the new apartment buildings where the site ended. "The trail must start here and go down to the fishing dock," he said.

"Mr. Cho will be happy," said Jessie. "I bet some of the people who move in here will like kayaking and canoeing." She stared out at the structures. It was hard to imagine what they'd look like when they were done.

Grandfather stopped the car at a stoplight near a sign for the new building. Benny sounded out the words. "'Live close to town. Stream views. Ex-er-cise room.'" He frowned. "Ugh. Exercise. Nope. I couldn't live there if you have to exercise."

"It's a choice," Henry explained. "Some people like to run or lift weights to stay healthy."

"And other people don't like running ever." Benny pointed at himself.

"What do you think they mean by stream view?" said Violet, looking back at the sign. "Do you think you could see the river from here? Even if you were way up in an apartment?"

Henry thought for a moment. The apartments were pretty far from the river. "I don't think so," he answered.

"It's weird that they are offering a view from here," said Jessie.

"Strange," Violet agreed.

"Odd," Henry said.

"What's another word for *weird*?" Benny whispered to Henry. Henry whispered back, and Benny said, "Bizarre!"

The light turned green, and Grandfather steered around the construction zone. Benny tried to think of more words that meant the same as *weird* until Grandfather reached the rental shack.

"Wacky," he said, as they gathered the supplies for the third sample.

Jessie and Henry put on the waders. Violet took a few pictures of the shack and the river in front of it.

"Wild," Benny said, holding the water scoop with two hands.

Violet took his photo.

"Unusual," Benny said, smiling. He gave Jessie the scoop. "I'm *unusually* good at thinking of words that mean the same thing," he said. "Get it? *Unusual* is like *weird* too!"

"A *rare* talent," Jessie took the net and prepared to go in the river.

Benny looked confused. Then he said, "Hey, that means *weird*, too, doesn't it!"

Henry and Jessie waded into the river to take their final soil sample. As they were moving around to break up the soil, a red pickup truck drove right through the parking lot and parked in front of Lazy River Rentals. A man in a blue baseball cap got out of the truck and stretched as though he had just woken up from a nap.

Watch ran up to Mr. Cho and put his feet on the man's knees.

Mr. Cho let out a yelp. "Shoo! Shoo!" he said, and Benny called Watch back to the riverbank.

"Sorry about him," Jessie called. "He shouldn't jump up like that."

"That's...okay," said Mr. Cho, catching his breath. "I...I just don't get along with dogs very well." Mr. Cho tipped his head to the side as though he had just noticed what the children were doing. "What are you children doing at the shop? And why are you two dancing in the river?"

"We're looking for mutant critters!" Benny called.

Mr. Cho looked even more confused.

Jessie stopped wiggling her feet to loosen up the soil. She held up the basin and motioned to the net Henry was holding. "We're collecting water samples for my science fair project," she explained.

"Like an experiment?" Mr. Cho said. "That sounds like an awful lot of work." He sat down on an old rusty chair next to the dock.

"We think it's important," said Violet. "We are

worried the water in the river might be polluted."

"Polluted?" said Mr. Cho, putting his feet up. "The Big Cleanup took care of all that. You children are wasting your time. The water here is as clean as ever."

"But if it isn't, aren't you worried about your business?" said Henry. "The other day you said not many people were coming to take lazy river rides."

Mr. Cho waved off the question. "The water is fine. Plus, pretty soon this river won't be my problem anymore."

With that, Mr. Cho stood up and went inside the Lazy River shack.

After Henry and Jessie were done collecting their sample, Jessie told Violet what critters she found. Then she filled a third jar with water and handed it to Benny.

He wrote a K for *kayak* and a *1* for the first sample.

As the children packed up their things, Violet said, "Mr. Cho was acting strange."

"I'd say," said Benny. "Who doesn't like dogs?" He gave Watch a nuzzle.

"You're right, Violet," Jessie said. "Mr. Cho didn't seem like he cared if the water in the river was dirty."

"So first Mrs. Fernando *was* worried about the river, but then she didn't want us to do our experiment," said Henry. "And now Mr. Cho doesn't seem worried at all, even though his business isn't doing well."

"What was that thing he said about the river not being his problem pretty soon?" Jessie said. "That was weird too."

"It's..." Benny tried to think of one more word for *weird*. "*Superweird!*"

***

Once the children were all packed up, Grandfather drove them to Jessie's school. She wanted to keep her supplies there so she could work on her project during her after-school club meetings. Grandfather helped the children carry their things inside. Then he took Watch home to start preparing lunch. The children would walk home together when they were done.

There were only a few other students in the science room.

"I have to analyze the data on my own," Jessie reminded Henry, Violet, and Benny. She took a large piece of paper from the science closet. "I'll make a chart."

Down one side, she wrote the locations where they collected the samples. Then next to each place she wrote: **Kinds of Critters**. Then **How Many Critters**. In the fourth column, she wrote: **Water, Color, and Smell**.

Jessie started with what they had found at the Lookout Café:

- 3 worms
- 4 crawdads
- 8 water bugs
- 1 snail
- 16 total

Then she checked out the water sample from the jar labeled *L1*. The color looked a little orange, mixed with light brown.

She sniffed the water. It smelled a tiny bit like rotten eggs, but not terrible rotten eggs. She wrote down that if a 1 was a great egg and a 10 was the worst egg ever, the water smelled like a 4.

Next, Jessie recorded what they had found at the fishing dock:

- 5 worms
- 6 crawdads
- 10 water bugs
- 4 snails
- 1 beetle
- 26 total

The water color in the *F1* jar was close to the color of the waterfall water—kind of orangey and brown. When Jessie held it to the light, Violet said it looked like Grandfather's favorite tea.

Benny smelled the fishing dock sample and reported, "This doesn't smell like tea. It's got that same eggy smell, like the water at the café." He smooshed up his face. "Yuck."

Jessie wrote down what Benny said, even though "eggy smell" wasn't a good scientific phrase. She knew that sulfur caused that smell. She wrote that down too.

The final sample was from the rental shack:

- 10 worms
- 12 crawdads

- 15 water bugs
- 8 snails
- 5 beetles
- 50 total

The water was clear blue. It was really pretty.

Benny sniffed it and said, "Oooh. What's better than rain and the ocean?" He thought about it. "This water smells like...rainbows!"

Jessie wrote that down because the water did smell very fresh.

When everything was recorded on the poster board, she held it up for Violet to take a photo. Jessie grinned as she pointed to the results. She wasn't sure what anything meant yet, but she was proud of her first day.

As the children were tidying up their workstation, Claudia walked into the science room. She was again wearing overalls and muddy boots. As soon as she saw the Aldens, she looked away and pretended not to notice them.

Jessie said, "Hi, Claudia. How's your project?"

"Oh, hi," Claudia said. "My project is fine." She noticed Jessie's chart. "So you're really doing the river project. Find anything interesting?"

"Yes," Jessie said, feeling proud. "Well, I'm not sure. I still need to compare these results to new samples later, but I think we're on to something." She looked at her siblings, and they all nodded.

"Well, good luck," said Claudia shortly. "You'll need it." With that, she set her notebook on a lab table and walked to the closet to get supplies for her own project.

"You wanted to be partners with her?" Benny whispered. "She doesn't seem very nice."

Jessie sighed. "I don't know what's gotten into her. She's never acted like this before."

Violet was looking at the notebook Claudia had left behind. The words *Vasquez Farms* were written in bold letters on the cover. "Is Claudia's last name Vasquez?" she asked.

"No, why?" Jessie asked. "Her last name is Tobin."

Violet raised her camera from around her neck. She had seen the name somewhere. She scrolled backward through their day, looking for something to jog her memory.

"Here!" she said. She pointed to a photo she had taken at the fishing dock. The small screen showed Henry untangling the fisherman's line across the river. Above him was a No Trespassing sign with the name Vasquez Farms across the top. Mrs. Vasquez owned one of the biggest farms in Greenfield. The children had often seen her at the farmers market selling potatoes and beans.

"That's where I found the pipe that was pumping something into the river," said Henry.

"Do you think Claudia has something to do with it?" asked Violet.

"I don't know," said Jessie. "But it is a strange coincidence."

"Oh, I know!" said Benny. "It's *curious*."

Jessie looked to the back of the classroom where Claudia was still choosing paper for her own project. "Curious indeed."

Two Problems

"We have three wonderful guests today!" Ms. Kennedy announced at the beginning of the next Science Fair Club meeting. "The science fair judges are here."

The night before, Jessie had stayed up late. She'd arranged the notes from her notebook, the data about the critters, and Violet's photos into a binder. The purple three-ring binder held everything they'd learned on Saturday.

When Team Alden visited the river again, she'd add new photos and data and compare the results. A lot could happen over a couple weeks.

Jessie knew her project was important. She couldn't wait to show Ms. Kennedy and the judges what she'd done so far.

The door opened, and three adults came into the room. Two men and one woman. They were the ones who would decide the science fair winner. They stopped to talk to Ms. Kennedy.

Jessie looked at Claudia. She had printed out papers and had them laid out in an orderly way. She looked really well prepared. Jessie tried not to be intimidated. Her project was good too.

"Your project looks great," said Jessie. "What are you working on?" The two still hadn't talked much since Claudia had decided to do her own project.

"A secret," Claudia said, shuffling her papers together.

"Are you still working by yourself?" Jessie asked.

"I have a partner," Claudia said. She clarified. "Not someone at school."

Jessie wondered if she meant Mrs. Vasquez from Vasquez Farms. But before she could ask, Ms. Kennedy called the class to attention.

"Students," the teacher said. "I want to introduce the judges."

Two Problems

The guests stood in a row in front of Ms. Kennedy's desk.

An older, short woman with thick black hair said, "My name is Carol Sterling. I'm an architect. I mostly design houses now." She looked around the classroom. "But, years ago, I designed this school."

The students applauded. The school was pretty amazing. It had big classrooms and a lot of windows. Jessie loved the library the most. There were skylights that cast sunbeams on the walls above the reading stations. Now every time she was there, she would think about Ms. Sterling.

A man with a mustache stepped forward. "I'm Peter Cooper." When he spoke, his mustache wiggled, making him seem friendly. "I'm an engineer. And I haven't designed any cool buildings. But like we say at my company, 'We Help You Build On.'"

Jessie had a lot of questions for Mr. Cooper. She knew that part of an engineer's job was to make sure things like water were protected. She wanted to ask him more about pollution.

Science Fair Sabotage

As if she knew Jessie had things to ask, Ms. Kennedy said, "There will be time for questions later. The judges will come speak to each of you individually."

The third judge was a tall, thin man with thick glasses and a long beard. He looked like a character out of one of Henry's favorite pirate novels.

"I'm James Blackstone," the man said. Jessie smiled to herself. It was a good pirate name. "I teach high school science in Silver City. I promise to be a fair judge." He began to move around the room. "I'm looking forward to hearing your ideas."

Ms. Sterling followed Mr. Blackstone. The two of them stopped at Claudia's lab table and began talking. They seemed very interested in Claudia's project. Jessie organized the samples and the binder on her table.

Before long, it was her turn to share her project with Ms. Sterling and Mr. Blackstone.

"Hi," Jessie began. She glanced over to where Mr. Cooper was still standing with Ms. Kennedy. He wasn't walking around with the others. Jessie wondered if she'd get a chance to talk to him too.

Two Problems

"What are you working on?" Mr. Blackstone asked. But Ms. Kennedy called out to Jessie from the front of the classroom.

"Oh, excuse me," she told the judges, not wanting to seem rude. "Ms. Kennedy needs me."

"We'll come back at the end, if there's time," Ms. Sterling told Jessie.

They moved on. Jessie left her binder on her desk and hurried over to her teacher.

"I want you to meet Mr. Cooper," Ms. Kennedy said.

"I hear you're working on an interesting project," the man said.

"I think so too." Jessie felt a little shy. "I'm studying the water quality in the Greenfield River," she told him, trying not to sound nervous.

"Very good!" he cheered. "As an engineer, I always need to pay close attention to things like water quality. If water issues aren't handled, a building project might be stopped or delayed."

Jessie felt like Mr. Cooper understood what she was doing and why. She couldn't wait to show him her binder and get his thoughts on what might be going on at the river.

"My research is on my desk," she told him.

"All of it?" he asked.

"Yes," Jessie said proudly. "Everything I've found so far is written in my binder."

He nodded and started to walk that way. Ms. Kennedy stopped Jessie and said, "I'm proud of your project, Jessie. Be sure to ask Mr. Cooper about his work too. He might have helpful information to share."

They talked for a minute about what kind of questions Jessie might ask. Then Jessie thanked her and hurried to meet up with Mr. Cooper.

"Purple," he said, putting a finger on her binder. "My favorite color."

"That's my sister's favorite color too," Jessie said. She wondered if she could volunteer for his company during summer vacation. She'd never thought of being an engineer. She'd like to know more about it.

"My brothers and my sister helped me take water samples from the river," she explained. "I counted up the bugs and critters in each sample, plus recorded the water's color and smell." Picking up her binder she said, "This was the first river visit. We'll go again next weekend to compare new samples."

"Sounds like a big project," Mr. Cooper said. He looked worried. "I was thinking you were doing something easier. Most of the other students are working with partners. You don't have a partner, do you?"

Jessie glanced at Claudia, who was chatting with the other judges. "I've got it under control," she said.

"All right," said Mr. Cooper. "Let's see what you've found so far."

Jessie smiled and opened her binder. But when she looked inside, all of the papers were gone. Jessie searched the lab table. She must have picked up the wrong binder.

"I'm so sorry," Jessie said. "I don't know where it all went. My papers must be around here somewhere."

"Hmm..." Mr. Cooper said, his mustache stuck in a frown. "It looks like you have a long way to go.

As we say at my company, you need to start with a good foundation to build on."

"I do..." said Jessie. "Or I did."

The man gave Jessie a sympathetic look. "You have chosen a big project. With only a couple weeks until the science fair, maybe you should try something else. Something simpler," he said. "Good luck."

And with that, the judge and all of the answers to Jessie's questions walked away.

***

That night in the boxcar, Jessie told Henry, Benny, and Violet about what had happened at Science Club. "I only left the table for a minute," she explained. "I've gone over the whole day in my head. I don't know when the pages might have gone missing."

"Are you sure you put the papers in the binder last night?" Henry asked. He had already asked her this question once before.

Jessie answered again, "I'm sure. I made sure it was all on the lab table just before the judges came over. Then *poof*! It disappeared!"

Two Problems

"Can I see the binder?" Benny asked. "Maybe there's a clue."

Jessie handed him the binder.

Benny got out a magnifying glass and started looking over the front cover. "Benny Alden is on the case," he said, slowly studying every inch.

Jessie sat down in her desk chair. She put her head down on the desk. "All that work," she groaned, "for nothing." With a long sigh, she said, "I think I have to drop out of the science fair."

"We can help you with another project," Henry said. "There's still time."

"We've lost all of our data from the river," Jessie said, not raising her head. "I don't want to start something new. I liked that project."

"We still have the jars showing the water color," Henry said. "If we think hard, we might remember what the bug counts were at each spot. Violet can print new photos. It shouldn't be too hard to make the chart again."

"The jars with the color of the water are a good start," said Jessie. "But they aren't very scientific."

Violet jumped up. "Hang on!" she shouted as she

dashed out of the boxcar. A minute later, she came back with her camera. "Remember, I took pictures during our critter count?" she said.

"Yes," said Jessie. "But we won't be able to get the right count using a photo."

"No," said Violet, shifting through images on her camera. "But we can get the right count from this." She stopped on the photo where Jessie was holding onto the chart she had made. The critter count was clear as day.

Jessie's eyes lit up. "We can remake the chart!" She gave her sister a big hug.

Then Benny said, "I found something! I found a clue!" He had been looking the binder over with his magnifying glass when he came across a piece of paper in the pocket.

"What does it say?" Jessie asked.

Benny pulled out the fortune-cookie-sized paper and read the note out loud. He used a deep, scary voice. "It says, 'Give up now. You will not win!'"

"Oh no!" said Violet. "Someone really *is* trying to stop your project."

Henry paced across the boxcar. "So now we have

two problems. First we need to figure out what is going on with the river. That's the experiment. Then we need to find out who doesn't want you to do your project. That's the mystery."

"Yay! A mystery!" said Benny. He paused. "Wait. There are always suspects in a mystery. Who are they?"

"I think Claudia is a suspect," said Jessie. "She has been acting weird, and she was in the room when my papers went missing."

"Speaking of acting weird," said Violet, "Mrs. Fernando and Mr. Cho were acting strange the other day. Maybe one of them knows something about what's going on at the river."

"Let's not forget about the pump we found at Vasquez Farms," said Henry. He reminded them of the name on Claudia's notebook. "Maybe the farm is putting something bad in the river, and Claudia knows about it."

"She did tell me her project was a secret. And that she has a secret partner," Jessie told them. "But I still don't think Claudia would do something so extreme."

Two Problems

"Uh-hum," Grandfather cleared his voice from the boxcar doorway. "I came to say good night. Don't stay out too late, children," he said.

But before he left, Jessie had a question for him. "Grandfather, do you know Mrs. Vasquez at all?" Grandfather had lived in Greenfield a long time, and it seemed like he knew just about everyone.

"Melinda Vasquez?" he said with a smile. "Well, of course! She was part of the Big Cleanup of the Greenfield River. She went to all the meetings. She talked to the neighbors. When people disagreed, she worked to convince them that the Big Cleanup was a good idea."

Grandfather put his hands on his hips. "Without Mrs. Vasquez, I'm afraid of what might have happened to Greenfield's water. She's a great lady." With that, Grandfather wished the children good night and went back into the house.

"It doesn't make sense," Jessie said, biting her bottom lip. "If Claudia is working with Mrs. Vasquez, what are they working on? And why doesn't Claudia seem to want to know more about what's going on in the river?"

"Hmm..." Benny said. He didn't have any answers. So he said, "There's no other word that means the same thing. So just hmm."

Rivers and Streams

On Saturday morning, Team Alden once again piled into Grandfather's car with all of their equipment. The children were excited to get another round of testing in so they could compare new samples to the first batch. And with only a week until the science fair, Jessie needed to make sure they did the tests the right way.

Grandfather parked at the Lookout Café, and everyone climbed out. Jessie looked at the patio. Today there were no customers sitting outside. Why weren't people enjoying the warm weather?

She wanted to go ask Mrs. Fernando what was going on. But then she remembered how upset she had been when they had tested under the patio.

"We better go a little farther downstream today," Jessie said.

"Have fun, children," Grandfather said. "Your chauffeur will be waiting here with a good book." Grandfather waved a paperback in the air.

The children followed the path at the back of the parking lot down to the river. As soon as Jessie got near the water, she understood why no one was sitting on the patio of the Lookout Café. The rainbow on the waterfall was gone. The water flowing over the falls was orange and brown. And from where she stood, Jessie guessed that the smell ranked at least an eight on the rotten-egg scale.

Benny walked to the water's edge then quickly turned around. "That is a lot of stink," he said. "*And* murk."

Henry put the waders on and moved out into the water. "The current isn't very strong. I had to be careful not to tip over last time. Now it's less like a river and more like a stream."

"Henry, what's the difference between a river and a stream?" Benny asked.

Henry pointed at the river. "A stream and a river

are both running water. Usually a river is wider and flows fast and is deeper than a stream."

"Stream. River. River. Stream," Benny repeated the words over and over to memorize them.

Jessie put on her waders and joined Henry in the water. She took a sample, and Benny plugged his nose and wrote L2 on the label.

Violet snapped photos as Jessie and Henry took their soil sample. When they were done, they counted the critters:

- 0 worms
- 1 crawdad
- 2 water bugs
- 1 clam
- 4 total

"That's a big change from last time," said Henry.

"I read that clams don't mind pollution," Jessie answered. "I don't even know if that one should count."

"There aren't as many birds or turtles around either," said Violet, lowering her camera.

"Let's see what we find at the other sites," said Henry. "I have a feeling something big is going on."

Together, the children walked back up to the Lookout Café parking lot. Mrs. Fernando was waiting for them, arms crossed. "Are you children still doing that experiment?"

"Don't worry," said Jessie. "We did our test farther down the river, away from the Lookout."

Mrs. Fernando shook her head. "That is not what I'm worried about." She motioned to the empty patio. "No one is here to scare away. The water has already done that!"

Jessie looked at the waterfall. From where the children were standing, it looked like brown sludge was flowing over the rocks.

"I thought you children were going to figure out who was doing this to the river?" said Mrs. Fernando. "This experiment isn't helping anyone."

"We think it will," Jessie said. "Eventually. We just need to collect all of the data first. Then present it at the science fair."

Mrs. Fernando sighed. "I don't know if I can wait that long," she said. "By then, the Lookout Café might be closed for good."

***

Rivers and Streams

Grandfather pulled into the parking lot for the fishing dock. This time, there was no one fishing on the dock. The water looked even browner and lower than it had by the Lookout Café. Jessie took a sample of the water, and she and Henry did their count:

- 2 worms
- 4 crawdads
- 6 water bugs
- 1 snail
- 0 water bugs
- 2 clams
- 15 total

"I don't understand what could cause such a big change so quickly," said Jessie. "The Greenfield River has been flowing for hundreds of years. I don't know if it has ever looked like this."

Violet took pictures of the scene. Benny wrote *F2* on the jar that Jessie passed to shore.

Henry had an idea. He stepped back into the water and started to wade across to the other side. This time the water only came up to his waist. Jessie followed.

Once they reached the other side, Henry bent down. He was looking for the pipe he'd found the last time they'd visited the fishing dock. Before long, he found it and listened. "The pump is turned off," he called. "There's no noise."

He followed the pipe up the riverbank.

"Henry, that's private property," said Jessie. "Come back."

"I just want to take a look," Henry said. But before he could take another step, a woman wearing overalls and muddy boots appeared at the top of the riverbank.

It was Mrs. Vasquez. "Oh my," she said. "Well, hello there!"

"Hello, Mrs. Vasquez," said Henry. He took a step back toward the river, but Mrs. Vasquez did not seem upset.

"I thought I heard some voices over here. Then I saw that nice car, and I thought it might be James Alden at the fishing dock."

"He's our grandfather," said Jessie.

"Oh, I see," said Mrs. Vasquez. "Well, then you must be Jessie."

Jessie was going to ask how Mrs. Vasquez knew her name, but instead she said, "Sorry we came onto your property. We were just working on my science fair experiment."

"Something is changing with the river," said Henry. "And we are trying to figure out what."

Mrs. Vasquez nodded. "So I've heard. And now I see it's true."

"Didn't you know about the water before this?" Jessie asked.

Mrs. Vasquez shook her head. "I'm afraid not. After all we did during the Big Cleanup, though, it's heartbreaking to see our town's river like this."

Henry and Jessie looked at each other. Mrs. Vasquez sounded very upset. Maybe Grandfather was right. Maybe she didn't have anything to do with the river changing colors.

"Do you see this grassy area between my field and the river?" she asked, helping the children up onto the top of the riverbank. "It may not look like much, but you are standing on ground that could make a whole lot of money if we planted crops here. Do you know why we don't?"

Henry shrugged.

Jessie said, "Is it because of the rules from the Big Cleanup?"

"Ding! Ding!" Mrs. Vasquez said. "This is called a buffer zone. It makes it so all of the water we use on our fields doesn't flow straight into the river. It has to go through this ground first."

"Why do you do that?" asked Henry.

"That way, the chemicals farmers like me use to help our crops grow don't find their way into our water," she said. "The soil here filters out all the bad stuff. When we found out how much of a difference just a little bit of grassy land makes, I helped make it a rule for all farmers around Greenfield."

"That must have upset a lot of farmers," said Jessie.

"It sure did," said Mrs. Vasquez. "It takes courage to take action at first. But eventually people saw that it was the right thing to do."

Jessie worked up her own courage. She said, "We found this pipe the other day, and it leads onto your land. Do you know what it does?"

Mrs. Vasquez smiled. "Is this what you wanted to know about?"

Jessie blushed. "We were worried you were pumping something into the water to make it change color."

"I'm afraid the answer is much more boring than that," said Mrs. Vasquez. "We aren't putting anything *into* the river. We are trying to pump *out* from the river." She bent low to show them how the pipe and pump worked. "I like to use natural sources to water the crops."

"That makes sense," said Jessie. "But the water level by the pump seems a bit low."

"At the café it's even lower," Henry added. "Could you be taking out too much water?"

Mrs. Vasquez shook her head. "This is such a small pipe. And the pump is small too. What we are doing barely changes the river at all."

"We're sorry we were suspicious," said Jessie.

"Oh, don't worry. I'm used to people being suspicious," said Mrs. Vasquez. "Just today, Mrs. Fernando from the Lookout Café called me. She thought I was polluting the river. I suppose it's what us farmers deserve for not taking better care for all those years. But I'm working to make things better.

I'm even working on a project right now with my niece. You know Claudia, right?"

"Claudia Tobin is your niece?" Jessie said.

"That's right. We're working to use even less water. And less water means less pollution."

"Is that her science fair project?" Jessie asked.

"Oh dear!" Mrs. Vasquez put a hand over her mouth. "Was it a secret?" She dropped her hand. "I am the worst at keeping secrets. You should never tell me anything! I'm such a chatterbox!"

Together, Jessie and Henry said good-bye to Mrs. Vasquez and waded back through the river. Jessie's mind raced with all they had just learned. Was that why Claudia had not wanted to work with her? Was she afraid that people would blame her aunt for any pollution they found? It made sense, but it still didn't explain why Claudia hadn't wanted to work with her at all.

As Grandfather drove the children around the construction site to take their last sample, Jessie thought they still had a long way to go to solving their mystery.

CHAPTER 7

Snooping and Shooing

Grandfather pulled into the parking lot of Lazy River Rentals. Mr. Cho's red pickup truck was not outside the shack, but there was another car in the parking lot. A Closed sign hung on the front door of the small building.

"Maybe someone took a river ride, and Mr. Cho went to pick them up," said Jessie.

"In this murky, mucky water?" asked Benny. "No way!"

But when the children came to the edge of the river, it did not look like the murky, mucky river they had seen at the fishing dock and at the Lookout. Instead, the water looked as clean as it had before, when Benny had said it smelled like "rainbows." In addition, the water looked clear and blue, and the water level had not gone down at all. If anything, the river seemed to swell even higher.

Still, Jessie needed to test the water for her project. She and Henry waded out into the river while Benny and Watch looked for fish in the water. Violet took photos of the birds.

They were just finishing collecting the water sample when the back door opened and closed on the rental shack. The wooden dock creaked as someone walked around the boardwalk toward the front. Whoever it was sounded like they were trying to be sneaky.

Benny, Watch, and Violet crept up to the building and rounded the corner. As they did, someone let out a scream.

"Mrs. Fernando!" said Violet. "What are you doing here?"

The woman straightened up. "Well, I...um...of course, I'm looking to take a river ride."

"In your work clothes?" Violet asked. She motioned to the serving uniform Mrs. Fernando

was wearing.

"Oh, this? You're right. How silly of me. I really must be going." And with that, Mrs. Fernando turned and hurried toward the other car in the parking lot.

"What was that about?" asked Jessie from the river.

Benny shrugged.

"It seemed like she was snooping around," said Violet. "Looking for something."

The children were taking their sample of the soil when a red pickup truck pulled up and a man in a blue hat stepped out. He did a big stretch as though he had just woken up from a nap.

Watch ran up to greet him, and Mr. Cho yelped and shooed him away. It took him a moment to see the children. "Oh, well, hello there," he said. "If you'd like to take another ride down the river, I'm afraid we're closed."

"Is that because you are worried about what's going on with the river?" asked Violet.

Mr. Cho looked confused. "River? What river is that?"

Science Fair Sabotage

Jessie and Henry exchanged a confused look. "This river?" said Jessie. "The water is changing color downstream."

"Oh, that?" said Mr. Cho. "No, I'm sure the water will clear up in no time." He waved his hand. "No, I've got some big plans coming up, and I need to do some...um...well...planning."

Jessie wondered what could be more important than finding out what was happening to the river. "We're here again to study the river water," she said. "It's for my science fair project."

"Yeah," said Benny. "We're going to find out who is making all the stink. And murk!"

"I'd have thought you'd have quit by now. I mean, with things going missing—" Mr. Cho paused. "I mean, the water is going down so much. There's not much to study."

"I think the water problems by the café make the project more important than ever," Jessie said. "Just because it's good here, doesn't mean there's not something big happening."

"It's serious," Benny added. "Important." He grinned. "Words don't have to mean exactly the

78

same thing, but can be used the same sometimes. Right, Henry?"

Henry ruffled Benny's hair. "Exactly."

"Correct!" Benny said.

Mr. Cho shifted his weight. "So you really think your project could make a difference?"

"Absolutely," said Jessie. "Something strange is going on. Everyone in Greenfield has a right to know."

Mr. Cho shook his head. "Well, as you can see, the water here is clear as ever," he said. "I think you are wasting your time. But I hope nothing goes wrong at the science fair." With that, he turned on his heel and went into the shack.

***

After Grandfather dropped the children off at school that afternoon, Jessie went straight to work on her science fair poster. She needed a new column. They hadn't measured the water level the week before. Not scientifically anyway. Now, it seemed important that the water level was going down.

"Put that the water was to my waist," Henry said,

tapping his hip. "Last week, that's where it was at the Lookout Café." He lowered his hand. "This time, it's down here."

Jessie sighed. "I wish we'd measured with a ruler. I can't imagine the judges are going to take Henry's hips seriously."

Henry wiggled. "Why not?"

"My results should be more scientific," Jessie said.

"I have an idea," said Violet. "I have photos of you and Henry standing in the river. If you date the photos on your poster, it will prove the water level is now lower by the café."

"That's great!" Jessie said. She turned the poster so everyone could see it. Henry, Violet, and Benny stood around. "Look here at the first column," Jessie said, as if she were presenting for the judges. She paused for them all to study the numbers.

"The numbers at the rental shack are great this week," Henry said. He read the results:

- 15 worms
- 13 crawdads
- 10 water bugs

- 12 snails
- 6 beetles
- 56 total

Violet added, "That's even better than before!"

"Everywhere else," said Henry, "the numbers have gone way down."

"And the water has gotten stinkier and murkier too," said Benny. "But at the shop, it still smells like rainbows."

Jessie nodded. "And that leads to the conclusion of my report..."

"Tell me!" said Benny. "What are you going to say?"

Jessie drew a quick map in her notebook.

"Here's the rental shack. Here's the fishing dock. And here's the café." She pointed to a spot between Lazy River Rentals and the fishing dock. "We need to focus on the flow of the river and where things start to change. Can you see what's between the shack and dock?"

"The construction site?" Violet asked.

"Exactly!" Jessie said. "I'm going to say that the problems in the river are clearly coming from the construction site."

"But who's making the trouble?" Benny asked.

"And why?" Henry wanted to know.

"Let's see if we can find out," Jessie said. "We've finished the experiment. Now it's time to solve the mystery."

CHAPTER 8

Behind the Wall

That night after supper, the children visited the construction site. They each rode their bikes, and Watch ran along on a leash next to Jessie.

"I think the fence gets bigger every time we see it," Benny said when they reached the site. "And taller too." He set his bike on a patch of grass and walked over to the fence. "There are no peek holes." He stood on his tiptoes then tried to look under, but there was no way to see inside.

"Maybe we can see something at the edge of the river," said Henry. The children walked down toward the fishing dock. But the fence extended all the way to the edge of the water. "I wish we would have brought the waders," said Jessie. "We could go around this fence and see what they're up to in there."

Just then, the children heard two men's voices from the other side of the fence line. It sounded like they were coming their way.

"Yes, this leads all the way to the river," a man's voice said. "Just like you wanted."

"And what about the river? The water is looking a little...different," said another voice. Jessie thought she recognized the man's voice.

The first man spoke again. "Yes. With any project, there are some issues that come up. But as I say, we just need to build on."

Jessie did not mean to eavesdrop, but it sounded like the men were coming toward where they were standing. And the second voice sounded very familiar. She pulled Watch to her to keep him calm.

"And what about the other issue?" the second voice asked. "Have you...uh...taken care of that?"

"Don't worry," said the first man. "They are only children. I have a plan."

It sounded like the two men were now just feet away. Watch burst away from Jessie's hold and pawed and barked at the fence.

One of the voices yelped at Watch's bark. The other said, "What was that?"

The second voice said, "I don't know. But let's get back."

With that, the children heard footsteps going back toward the apartment buildings.

"One of those voices sounded familiar," said Benny.

"I thought so too," said Jessie, but she still couldn't figure out from where.

"Let's follow them," said Henry. "We need to figure out what they're building in there."

Henry led the way, as the children walked along the fence line. About every fifty feet, there was a sign for the construction company: BO CONSTRUCTION.

"I wonder who Bo is," said Benny. "Do you think that was who was talking? Jessie, do you know any Bos?"

Jessie shook her head. "I don't think so."

"BO could also be someone's initials," said Henry.

Benny thought about this. He started naming all the different names he could think of with the initials BO. "Do you know Bob Oak? Billy Oatmeal? Oh! What about Becky Olson?" He paused. "There are a lot of names that start with those letters."

Near the new apartment buildings, under the sign that announced the exercise room and the stream view, the children stopped. Someone had left a gate slightly open.

"Those men must have come out here," said Jessie.

"We can't trespass," Henry warned.

"But we can look, right?" Benny said. "Looking isn't against the law."

Henry smirked. "Looking is totally legal." He let Benny peak through the gate first.

"I knew it!" Benny said. "This is a stream," he said to the others. "It's like a river, only smaller."

Henry asked, "I think I understand. But can you explain?"

"I've been thinking a lot about words lately," Benny said. "The apartment sign says there's a

stream view. A stream is a *like* a river, but it's also *not* a river."

Henry stared up at the construction sign. "We thought the sign meant a river view, but the apartments are too far away from the river," he said.

"The poster says exactly what it means!" Benny said. He pointed at the water flowing close to the buildings. "BO Construction is making a stream!" He sang, "Stream views for the apartments!" Then in a lower voice. "Not river views. Don't be confused."

"This new stream is taking water out of the river," Jessie said. "That's why the water is lower at the farm and the café. Some of the water is here now."

"And from what that man said, the construction made the pollution," Henry added. "Probably from all the dirt they had to move!"

"So they weren't building a walking path at all," said Jessie.

"No," said Henry. "It was a different type of pathway."

Jessie thought back to the map of Greenfield she

had looked at for her project. She looked at where the stream was headed. "This probably connects to the Silver River on the other side of town," she said. "Why would anyone want that?"

"I don't know," said Henry. "But I have a feeling whoever it is doesn't want your project getting in the way."

The Big Day

On the day of the science fair, Grandfather brought Henry, Jessie, Violet, Benny, and Watch to the local community center.

"Don't you want to come in, Grandfather?" said Benny.

"Well, of course I do," Grandfather said. "But somebody has to keep an eye on Watch. I couldn't bear to leave him home alone on a beautiful day like this."

"That's right," said Benny. "Watch is a part of Team Alden too!"

The children said good-bye to Grandfather and Watch and went inside the community center. The building was filled with students and parents from

Greenfield and the surrounding area.

In the gymnasium, poster boards from all of the students' projects were being set up. There were hundreds on display.

One project had a row of vegetables connected with wires and a lit-up lightbulb. Another showed an experiment measuring the best way to grow potted pants. Still another was a volcano made of paper-mache.

"Wow," said Benny. "You could have made something explode for your project, Jessie!"

Jessie smiled. "We can do that sometime at home," she said. "Right now, I'm just worried about *my* project." She had stayed up late the night before, making sure everything was perfect. She'd added the information about the new stream, and about how the construction was causing pollution. "I just wish we knew who was behind the new stream and why."

"We can figure out the mystery later," said Henry. "Right now, let's focus on making sure you win the science fair."

The children reached the table with Jessie's

name on it. Violet laid out a neatly pressed purple tablecloth. Jessie placed her binder on top and set up the poster board. Henry set out the water samples they had taken, showing how the water had changed color. Benny propped up the net they had used to take samples next to the table. When they were done, Violet said, "It's very impressive. I think you have a really good chance, Jessie."

"What's going on over there?" Benny said. He pointed to a crowd gathered around one of the projects in the next row. Standing in front of the crowd was Claudia Tobin. At the top of her board were the words, "Safe Farming for the Environment."

"Claudia's project looks good too," said Violet. "I feel kind of bad that we thought she might be doing something to the river."

"I do too," said Jessie. But part of her still wanted to know why Claudia had decided not to work with her. "Maybe I should go wish her luck."

Just then, a man at the front of the gymnasium began speaking into a microphone. It was Mr. Cooper, the engineer judge with a mustache.

The Big Day

"Welcome to the regional science fair," Mr. Cooper said. "Thank you, all, for your hard work in creating a positive place for research. You are all the future scientists of the world. At this time, I have to ask that everyone leave the gymnasium. There will be a short period of time for the judges to look at the displays and prepare questions before the presentations begin. I ask for your patience, as we have a lot of projects to evaluate."

"Why don't we go to the concession stand?" said Henry.

"Yay!" said Benny. "Maybe we can get something for Watch to eat too."

Jessie paused. The last time she had left her project, her data had gone missing. "Let's wait for the crowd to leave first," she said.

The Aldens stood as a stream of people passed by. Suddenly, someone screamed from the row in front of Jessie's, and a stream of pink liquid shot into the air, splashing over the crowd.

"The volcano! It erupted!" Benny said, watching the liquid fly through the air. "We are *definitely* doing that at home, Jessie."

The Big Day

Next to the volcano, a girl Jessie's age looked on in horror. "How could it explode?" she said. "I haven't even added the vinegar!"

A woman who must have been the girl's mother led her out of the gymnasium crying. Before long, it was only the Aldens, the judges, and a janitor cleaning up the mess from the exploded volcano. The man wore a blue janitor's uniform with a blue baseball cap pulled down over his eyes.

"I think we'd better go," said Henry.

Jessie still didn't feel good about leaving her experiment, but she had no other choice. She followed her siblings out of the gymnasium.

At the concession stand, the children placed their orders. As they waited for their food, they saw a familiar face.

"Mrs. Fernando?" said Jessie. "What are you doing here?"

"I came to see your project," Mrs. Fernando said. "And wish you luck."

"But we thought you were mad at us!" said Benny.

Mrs. Fernando sighed. "Yes, I can see how you might have thought that. I am sorry. It's just, seeing you children doing that experiment...it... reminded me of what happened during the Big Cleanup. People saw the river being tested, and they got scared. I wanted to figure out what was really going on."

"We are sorry we scared your customers," said Jessie. "I could have thought about that more when I planned my experiment."

Mrs. Fernando shook her head. "No, no. I shouldn't have dismissed your project. To find out what's going on, you need proof. And your project is all the proof we have."

"Is that what you were doing at Mr. Cho's?" asked Violet. "Looking for proof?"

Mrs. Fernando sighed. "That man is always looking for a shortcut of some kind. I just knew he had something to do with the whole thing. But I couldn't find anything to prove it."

"We haven't put all the pieces together yet, either," said Jessie. "But I know we will."

"I have little doubt about that," said Mrs. Fernando with a kind smile. "Good luck."

The Aldens' order came up at the counter, and

the children said good-bye to Mrs. Fernando. As they looked for a place to sit, Jessie noticed another familiar face.

Claudia was sitting alone at a table.

"I'll catch up with you guys in a little bit," Jessie said. "I'm going to go say good luck to Claudia."

Jessie went over to Claudia's table. "Hi," she said. "I just want to say good luck today. Not that you will need it."

"Thanks," said Claudia.

Jessie thought she seemed sad. "Where is your partner?" she asked.

Claudia sighed. "She couldn't make it. She wanted to, but with the harvest coming up, she had too much to do."

"Sorry," said Jessie. "Your project looks great."

"So does yours," said Claudia. "Did your brothers and sister help you?"

Jessie nodded. "They helped me put it all together." She thought for a moment about Claudia's question, then added, "Is that why you didn't want to be my partner?"

Claudia sighed. "That was part of it," she said.

"I think I was just hurt because it seemed like you had already started without me. I was looking forward to being a team."

"I'm sorry I didn't include you from the start," said Jessie. "Maybe next time we can work together. After all, our projects are pretty similar."

"I would like that," said Claudia.

Just then, a voice came over the speaker, inviting everyone back into the gymnasium for the beginning of presentations.

"Well, we can start right now," said Jessie. Together, they went with Henry, Violet, and Benny back into the gymnasium.

But when they reached the table with the purple tablecloth, Jessie's poster and binder were gone.

The Man in the Blue Hat

"How could this have happened?" said Jessie.

The children searched under the table. They traveled up and down the aisle looking for the poster board. There was no sign of it. All of the other projects looked like they were intact.

"Maybe the judges moved your poster," said Henry.

"That's right," said Violet. "Maybe yours was so good they moved it somewhere special."

Jessie had a bad feeling. She knew someone had been trying to stop her project, but she'd thought it would be safe in the gymnasium with the judges.

"The judges will know what to do," said Claudia. "I don't see Ms. Sterling or Mr. Blackstone, but there's Mr. Cooper."

Mr. Cooper was standing with Ms. Kennedy.

"Mr. Cooper, my project has gone missing," said Jessie.

"We think someone stole it!" said Benny.

"Oh my," said Mr. Cooper. "Are you sure you didn't misplace it?"

"Yes," said Jessie. "It was all set up for the judges, and when we came back, it was missing."

"Well, I don't know what to say," said Mr. Cooper. "We judges were the only ones allowed inside during the last session. Surely you don't think one of us took it?"

Jessie didn't know quite what to say.

"There was one other person in the gymnasium," said Violet. "What about the janitor?"

"Janitor?" asked Mr. Cooper. "I did not see any janitor."

"That's right," said Ms. Kennedy. "One of my students had an unfortunate...explosion before the break. There was a man here helping to clean up the mess."

The Aldens looked around for the man who

had been pushing the mop bucket around the gymnasium. "Over there," said Henry, pointing across the crowded gymnasium. "I see his blue hat!"

"This isn't necessary..." Mr. Cooper began. "I assure you—"

But the children were already off to ask the man if he had seen anything. As soon as the man saw them moving through the crowd, though, he tipped over his mop bucket and took off running out of the gymnasium, a big plastic bag over his shoulder.

Henry led the way as the children followed the man out of the gymnasium. He took a right and went out the front doors. Before the children could catch up, they heard a yelp and a crash from outside.

Outside, Grandfather and Watch were standing by a park bench. The man was on the ground, holding his ankle, and Watch was playfully licking the man's face. The bag had split open, revealing what was left of Jessie's poster board, which was covered in pink goo.

"Get him away, please," said the man, taking off his hat and throwing it to try to shoo Watch away.

"I don't like dogs!"

"Mr. Cho?" said Jessie. "You were the one trying to ruin my project?"

With Watch finally off of him, Mr. Cho sat up and brushed himself off. Then he sighed.

"That's right," he said. "I was afraid your project would end the construction on the river."

"But why would you want to change the river?" said Benny. "Mutant fishes can't be good for your business."

Mr. Cho looked confused, but he continued anyway. "Nobody wanted to come to my business. I thought if I made the lazy river longer, more people would want to come visit. The only way to do that was to go around the waterfall at the Lookout Café. So I worked with a construction company to make it happen."

"So it was you the other night at the construction site," said Jessie. "I knew I recognized your voice."

"And that's why you weren't worried about the river," said Henry. "You were just planning to make a new one!"

Jessie thought about what they were hearing.

"But you couldn't have been the one who sabotaged my experiment," she said. "You weren't in the science room when my data went missing. You must have been working with someone else."

Just then, Mr. Cooper and the rest of the judges came out of the community center.

"What's going on out—" Mr. Cooper stopped when he saw Mr. Cho on the ground.

"Mr. Cho...What are you doing out here?" he said.

"We just found out that Mr. Cho was trying to ruin Jessie's experiment!" said Henry. "And he is working with someone else."

"Well," Ms. Kennedy said. "Do you have any proof of this? As scientists, we need proof of such things."

"That's right," said Mr. Cooper. "As we say at my company, you need facts to build on."

Jessie looked at Mr. Cooper. She had heard him use that phrase many times before. "Build On!" she said. "Those are the letters from the sign: *BO*!"

"Mr. Cooper, is your company BO Construction?" asked Henry.

Mr. Cooper looked around nervously but nodded.

"It wasn't initials or a man named Bo after all," said Benny. "It was a motto! Right, Jessie?"

"That's right, Benny," said Jessie. "And it means that Mr. Cooper's company is the one polluting the Greenfield River."

"I have a feeling you were also the one working to sabotage Jessie's project," said Henry, pulling Jessie's mushy poster board out of the trash bag.

"What do you have to say for yourself, Mr. Cooper?" asked Ms. Kennedy.

Mr. Cooper pointed down at Mr. Cho. "It was his idea!"

"Don't blame me," Mr. Cho said, standing up.

"You wanted a river that didn't stop at the waterfall," said Mr. Cooper. "You loved the idea."

"You wanted a view for your apartments!" Mr. Cho said, standing very close to Mr. Cooper. "And you couldn't see the river from your buildings."

"The stream would have been good for both of us!" Mr. Cooper told Mr. Cho.

"That may be," said Claudia. "But that does not

mean you can pollute the river in the process."

"We didn't mean for the water level to go down," Mr. Cooper said. "We thought that there was enough water for both the big river and the little stream."

Ms. Kennedy looked from Jessie to Claudia. Then, she made an announcement. "Mr. Cooper is no longer a judge for the science fair."

Before long, the mayor of Greenfield and the chief of police came to talk to Mr. Cooper. Mr. Cho went with them to the police station. They wanted to ask him questions about the stream plans.

After things were sorted out, Ms. Kennedy came up to Jessie. "I'm sorry," she said. "But you can only present with a board."

Jessie looked at her board. It was covered in pink goo from the volcano explosion.

Claudia stepped up. "She can present with me."

"Are you sure?" Jessie asked. "I don't want to hurt your chances of winning."

Claudia smiled. "We're partners, remember?"

"All right," said Ms. Kennedy. "I will give you both some time to prepare. You will be the last ones to present."

A little while later, it was Claudia and Jessie's turn. Claudia talked about all of the ways farmers had worked to lower their pollution since the Big Cleanup, and ways that could still be improved. Jessie told the judges all about how the number of critters in the Greenfield River was going down, and how the water was changing because of the construction.

"In conclusion," Jessie said, "the biggest thing I learned from this project was how many of us need the river. It's not only the tiny critters you can barely see. Having good water is important for the fish that eat those critters, and for the birds that eat the fish. It's important for the fisher and the kayaker and the farmer. But it's also important to the Lookout Café, and to the whole town of Greenfield. I hope—"

Jessie looked at Claudia, and at her brothers and sister. "We hope that our experiment will show that there are problems with the river, but when we work together, we can make change for the better."

The crowd around Claudia's project erupted in

applause as Jessie finished her speech.

When the room quieted down again, Ms. Kennedy held up the science fair trophies. "Our two judges have decided on a winner!"

First, she announced that a boy with a spider web project was the runner-up.

Jessie and Claudia held hands, hoping that she'd announce them next.

"This year, we have a new champion..." Ms. Kennedy announced.

Jessie and Claudia looked at each other nervously.

"And an old champion," Ms. Kennedy continued. "Jessie Alden and Claudia Tobin are the winners! Their project has already made a difference. And I have a feeling it will continue to do so in the weeks and months ahead."

Jessie and Claudia went to the front of the gymnasium to collect the trophy. Jessie thanked her family, and Claudia thanked Mrs. Vasquez for helping her with her project. Then the two stood by their poster and answered questions about the river and what could be done to clean it up.

The Man in the Blue Hat

When it was time to go, Mrs. Fernando came to the booth with a platter of cookies. "Guess what?" she asked.

"Oh, I want to guess," Benny said. He looked at the platter. "Are the cookies a clue?"

Mrs. Fernando laughed. She explained, "I didn't want to jinx it before you won. But we've decided to add a new dessert to the Lookout Café menu. These are Science Fair Fudge Sticks, to thank you for figuring out what was wrong with the river." The cookies were vanilla, covered in chocolate.

Benny took one. "I love the science fair. I can't wait until I'm old enough to do a project of my own."

Mrs. Fernando grinned and gave Benny a second treat. She turned to the trophy. "Congratulations, Jessie. And to you too, Claudia. Plus, all the Aldens. You all deserve the prize!"

Benny took a bite of his science fair cookie and licked his lips. "This is the best cookie I've ever had," he said. Then he asked Henry, "What's another word for *yummy*?"

Turn the page to read a
sneak preview of

THE SKELETON
KEY MYSTERY

the new
Boxcar Children mystery!

"'I run all day and never walk. I tell you something, but I don't talk.'" Benny Alden slowly sounded out each word on the piece of paper.

"Good job, Benny," said Jessie. She was twelve and knew how much her six-year-old brother loved learning to read.

Violet snapped a picture of the page with her camera. Violet was ten, and she always photographed the children's adventures—even the spooky ones. "Now we just have to figure out what it means," she said.

"Something that runs without walking...and tells us something without talking. Those are clues," said Henry. At fourteen, he was the oldest of the Alden children. He liked solving problems. "The answer must be hidden somewhere in this room."

Benny looked around with his flashlight. The room had once been a study. But it seemed as though no one had used it in years. There was a clutter of old objects. And plenty of cobwebs. The single window had been painted over, and the only light came from a dim lamp in a corner. In the opposite corner, a wooden box shaped like a coffin leaned against the wall.

Violet searched along a shelf stuffed with old books and trinkets. "There are so many places for things to hide," she said. "The answer to the riddle could be anywhere."

Suddenly, Violet jumped. Out of the corner of her eye, she had seen something move.

"Are you okay?" Jessie asked.

Violet turned and let out a sigh of relief. In a large, dusty mirror, she saw her reflection looking back at her. "Yes," she said. "This room is full of surprises."

Jessie looked up at the strange clock on the wall. It was a made of metal and shaped like a skull. "We only have ten minutes left," she said. "We need to hurry!"

"Oh!" said Henry.

"What is it?" asked Violet. "Did something happen?"

Henry shined his light toward the strange clock. "I think I figured out the riddle," he said. "Something that runs and never walks..."

It took Jessie a moment. Then she understood. "A clock runs but never walks!" she said. "And it tells us the time without saying a word!"

The children gathered around the strange clock. Its eyes glowed red. Cobwebs hung from all sides.

"It's too high to reach," said Violet. "Even for you, Henry."

"Benny, come sit on my shoulders," Henry said.

Benny looked up at the clock and gulped. "Are—are you sure that's the answer to the clue?" he asked.

"I'm sure," said Henry. "Come on. Let's check it out."

Benny climbed onto Henry's shoulders, and Henry lifted him up to the clock.

"I don't see anything," said Benny.

"Feel inside the mouth," said Henry. "There could be something in there."

"The mouth?!" said Benny. "What if it tries to bite me?"

"The skull isn't alive," said Henry. "It can't bite you."

Benny closed his eyes and looked away. Slowly, he reached his fingers into the clock. Then he yanked his hand away and squealed.

"What is it?" asked Jessie.

"It felt like a tooth!" said Benny.

"Benny, we need to hurry," said Violet.

"Okay, I'll grab it this time." Benny reached back in, quickly this time, and pulled out a small flashlight. He turned it on, and a purple glow appeared.

"A purple light!" cried Violet. "How pretty!" Violet loved the color purple. She had purple ribbons tied on her pigtails and was wearing purple sneakers.

Benny handed the flashlight to Henry.

"This is called a black light," said Henry. "Black lights can show things that are fluorescent."

"What in the world does that mean?" asked Violet.

"Things that are fluorescent absorb ultraviolet light," said Jessie. "It makes them glow."

"So some things might glow if we point the black

light at them?" asked Violet.

"That's right," said Henry. "Benny, reach back in there. Maybe there is a clue about the black light."

Benny sighed and reached into the skull's mouth once more. This time, he pulled out a folded piece of paper and handed it to Jessie. Henry lowered him to the floor.

"That was very brave," said Jessie. "Because you faced your fears, we found two clues to help us get out of here."

"Fears?" said Benny, blushing. "I wasn't afraid. I just—I didn't want to upset the cobwebs."

Jessie smiled at her little brother. She quickly unfolded the paper and handed it to him. "Well, either way, you get to tell us what the next clue says."

Benny sounded out the words on the page. "'I'm like a garden of blossoms bright. That only blooms in dark of night.'"

"I wonder what that could be," said Violet.

The Aldens shined their lights around the room, and Henry started listing what he saw. "There are books, an old lamp, a desk, a vase—"

"A coffin," said Benny, turning back to the big

box in the corner. "And there's probably a skeleton inside of that."

"Oh Benny, don't let your imagination get the best of you," said Jessie. "It's just for show. There's nothing inside." Jessie knocked on the box to prove that it was hollow, but Benny still wasn't so sure.

"I have an idea," said Violet. "What if the answer is flowers?"

"Good thinking, Violet," said Henry. "Let's turn off our flashlights and see if the flowers in the vase shine in the black light."

Benny was still eyeing the coffin in the corner of the room. "Are you sure we have to turn off our lights?" he said. "Maybe it's not the flowers after all."

"It will be fine," said Jessie. She grabbed Benny's hand, and all the children shut off their lights. Henry held up the black light to the vase.

"It's all dark." Violet frowned. "No bright blooms anywhere."

"Maybe we should turn our flashlights back on and think some more," said Benny.

"Let's look around the room first," said Jessie,

squeezing Benny's hand. "According to the clue, something should be glowing."

The children looked all around. Violet was the first to look up. "There are stars on the ceiling!" she said.

Sure enough, with the black light, the ceiling was glowing like the night sky.

"A garden that blooms at night—stars!" said Jessie. "Good eyes, Violet."

Henry panned the light across the ceiling. "They must be made of some kind of special paint," he said.

"We need to figure out what the clue means," said Jessie. "We only have a few minutes before we're stuck in here!"

Henry studied the glowing stars. With his finger, he traced the shape that the brightest ones made. "It's like a constellation," he said.

"What's that?" asked Benny.

"A constellation is a shape made by the brightest stars," Jessie explained.

Benny tilted his head. "Oh, I see. It looks like the letter T!"

"Does that mean we need to look for something

that starts with that letter?" asked Violet. She studied the room. "*T* could stand for *table, tray, teacup, typewriter*. Now that I think of it, there are a lot of things that start with *T*."

Henry squinted at the shape. "I don't think it's a T. I think it's an arrow!"

Benny clicked on his light and guided it along the arrow and across the room. The beam came to rest on the coffin in the corner. "I knew there was something in there!" he said. Benny stepped behind Jessie.

The other children turned on their flashlights and pointed them at the wooden box. Slowly, Henry walked over. As he pulled on the cover, the hinges gave an eerie creak. Finally, Henry yanked open the cover and shined his flashlight inside.

"There's nothing here!" he said.

"See, Benny? Nothing to worry about," said Jessie.

"Except we need to figure out how to get out of here!" said Violet. "We don't have much time left."

Henry, Jessie, and Violet searched around the old coffin. The inside was smooth and lined with silk. Henry felt along the edges. "I don't feel anything hidden inside," he said.

"Maybe we misread the clue," said Jessie.

Benny was still standing away from the coffin. He noticed something on the open cover. "There's a pocket!" he said.

Jessie looked at the lid, where there was a small pouch. "Good eyes, Benny," she said, reaching inside.

"Hurry!" said Benny, wringing his hands. "We have less than a minute to get out!"

"There's something in here!" said Jessie. She pulled out a long, metal object with a fancy-looking handle.

"It's the skeleton key!" Benny cried.

The children ran to the entrance. Jessie jiggled the key into the lock, and the heavy door swung open. The Aldens rushed out as the room went black.

***

"Just in time!" said a tall man standing on the other side of the door. James Alden smiled at his four grandchildren.

"I'll say!" said Henry. "That was a close call!"

"Your grandchildren are indeed terrific mystery

solvers, James! Just as you described them." Verónica applauded along with her daughter, Maru.

Verónica was a friend of Grandfather's. The Aldens were staying with her and Maru as they visited the town of Hammond Hills. It was October in the Northeast, and the rolling hills of Appalachia were alive with the bright colors of autumn. People had come from miles around to look at the brilliant leaves and enjoy fall activities.

"I'm glad you were able to solve my escape room!" said Maru. "Were the riddles hard to figure out?"

"The riddles were very clever," said Jessie.

"But we all worked together to solve them," said Violet.

"I was the clue reader!" said Benny, smiling proudly.

Henry nodded.

"We used to live in one room," said Henry. "And we escaped from it as well!"

GERTRUDE CHANDLER WARNER discovered when she was teaching that many readers who like an exciting story could find no books that were both easy and fun to read. She decided to try to meet this need, and her first book, *The Boxcar Children*, quickly proved she had succeeded.

Miss Warner drew on her own experiences to write the mystery. As a child she spent hours watching trains go by on the tracks opposite her family home. She often dreamed about what it would be like to set up housekeeping in a caboose or freight car—the situation the Alden children find themselves in.

While the mystery element is central to each of Miss Warner's books, she never thought of them as strictly juvenile mysteries. She liked to stress the Aldens' independence and resourcefulness and their solid New England devotion to using up and making do. The Aldens go about most of their adventures with as little adult supervision as possible—something else that delights young readers.

Miss Warner lived in Putnam, Connecticut, until her death in 1979. During her lifetime, she received hundreds of letters from girls and boys telling her how much they liked her books.